For my nieces and nephews.

For all the storytellers I've
learned from across the world
and those holding this book.

Thank you for dreaming and
inspiring me to do the same.

ISBN: 978-1-7364038-8-4
Imprint: Independently published

Nia's Question

By Adelia Davis

Illustrations by Zoe Black

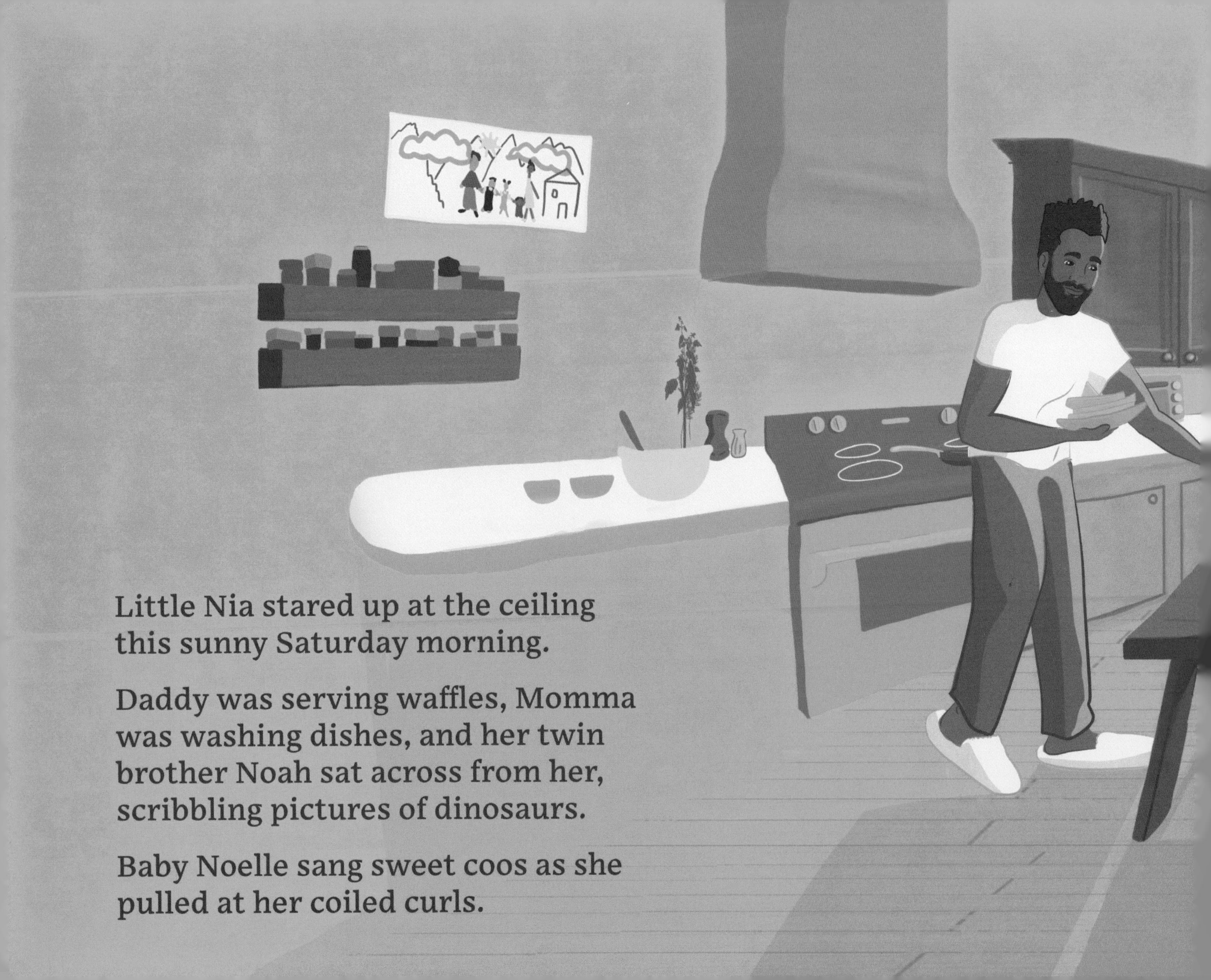

Little Nia stared up at the ceiling this sunny Saturday morning.

Daddy was serving waffles, Momma was washing dishes, and her twin brother Noah sat across from her, scribbling pictures of dinosaurs.

Baby Noelle sang sweet coos as she pulled at her coiled curls.

"Daddy, where is God?" Nia asked while still searching the ceiling. Daddy froze as he was about to place a waffle on Noah's plate.

"That's a great question, my love. Why don't you ask God?" he said with a gentle smile.

"Of course! I will ask God!" Nia thought with excitement.

She climbed down from her chair when no one was looking, and started her search in their backyard.

In the backyard, Nia saw the swing set where she and Noah became superheroes after school. She saw the big fruit tree and thought of getting full from its treats. Momma's special purple flowers had bloomed, because daddy cares for them each day.

"God, where are you?" Nia whispered in her head.

"I am all around you."

Nia's eyes widened, and she grinned as she thought up an idea.

She wandered out of her backyard and walked and walked and walked until she was on the other side of town.

The houses on this block looked like a big gust of wind had threatened to blow them down.

She didn't see any flowers, and someone had painted DIE on the wall of an apartment building.

As Nia was beginning to feel afraid, a group of kids her age ran past her playing cops and robbers.

"God, where are you?" Nia whispered in her head.

"I am all around you."

This gave Nia the courage to *skip and skip and skip* until she ended up at the edge of a busy street.

She was surrounded by tall buildings, and lots of people hurried past her. She saw flashing neon lights in all sizes and shop windows selling any and everything.

"God, where are you?"
Nia whispered in
her head.
"I am all around you."

Nia giggled with relief and began to **run and run and run** until she saw houses made of tin, smelled grilling meat, and heard loud music she couldn't understand.

She smiled back at the little girls watching her from their doorstep, as a group of boys played soccer in their dirt yard.

"God, where are you?"
Nia whispered in her head.

"I am all around you."

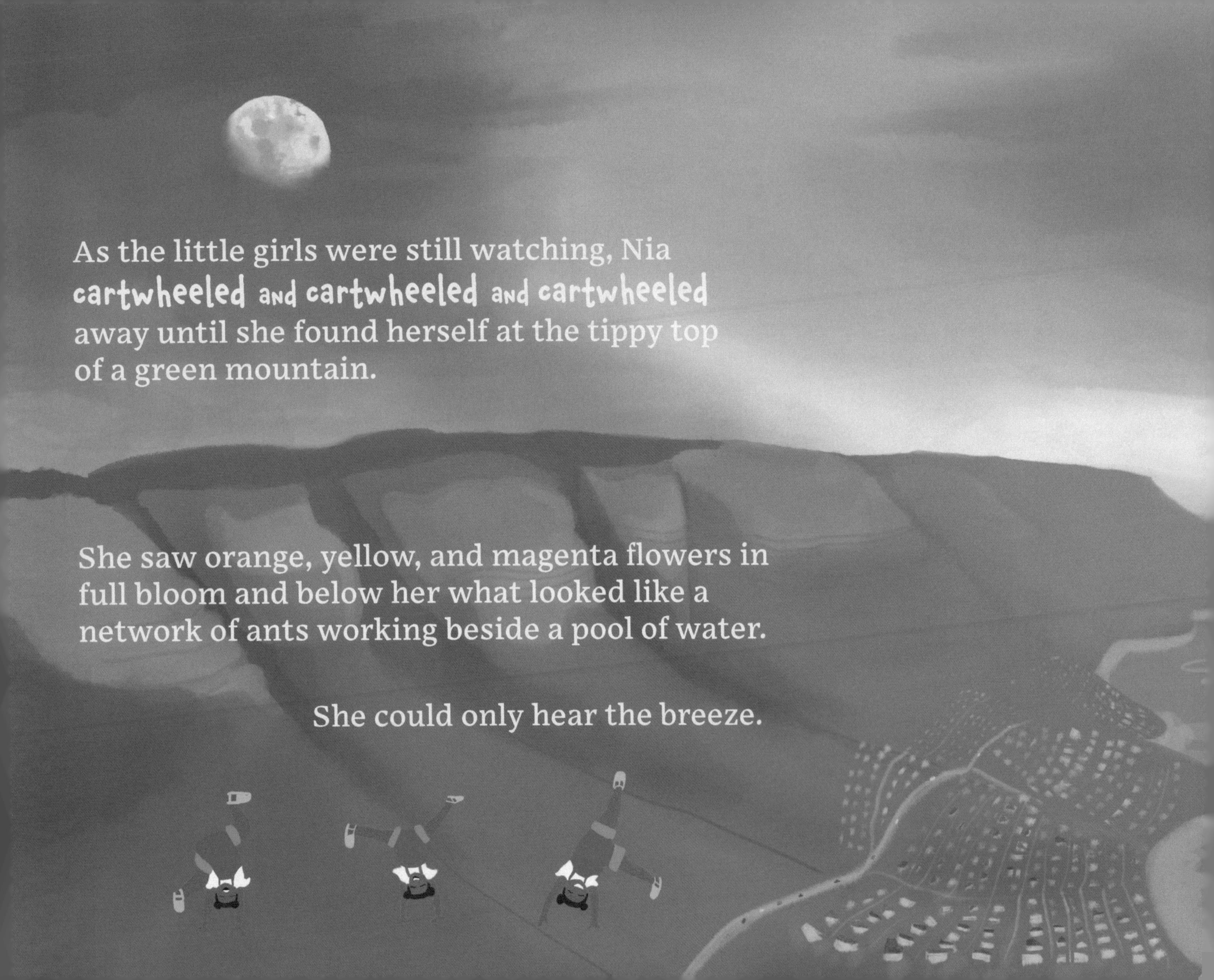

As the little girls were still watching, Nia **cartwheeled and cartwheeled and cartwheeled** away until she found herself at the tippy top of a green mountain.

She saw orange, yellow, and magenta flowers in full bloom and below her what looked like a network of ants working beside a pool of water.

She could only hear the breeze.

"God, where are you?"
Nia whispered in her head.
"I am all around you."

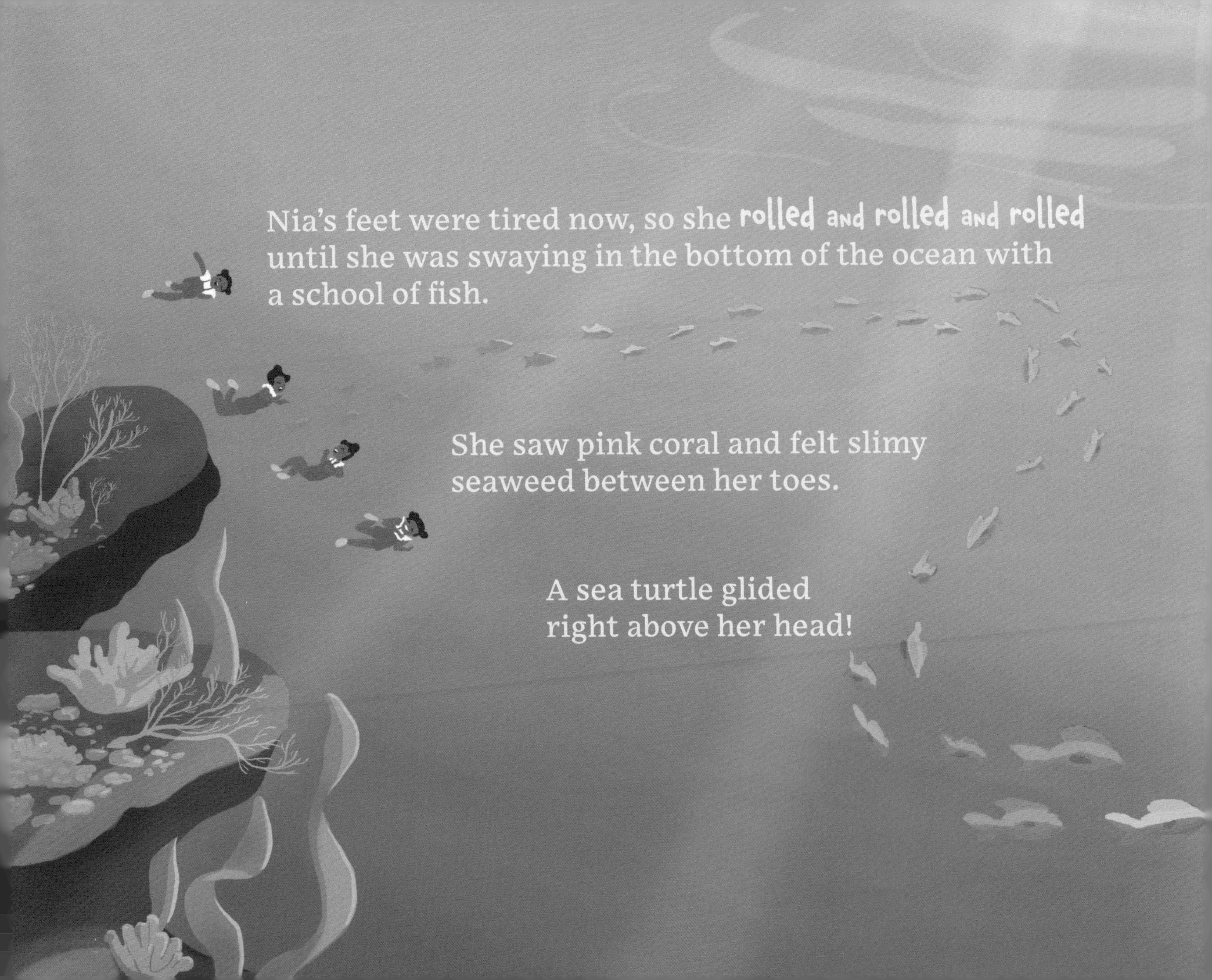

Nia's feet were tired now, so she **rolled and rolled and rolled** until she was swaying in the bottom of the ocean with a school of fish.

She saw pink coral and felt slimy seaweed between her toes.

A sea turtle glided right above her head!

"God, where are you?"
Nia whispered in her head.
"I am all around you."

Nia Swam and Swam and Swam until she couldn't swim anymore. Stars twinkled and glistened in the darkness around her.

She saw round, colorful balls off in the distance, but she couldn't hear anything.

She slowly closed her big, brown eyes...

"God, where are you?"
Nia whispered in her head.

"I am all around you."

When Nia opened her eyes, she was in her bathtub at home.

Momma lifted her out of the water and wrapped a warm, fuzzy towel around her. She held her up to the mirror and smiled at her reflection.

"God, where are you?"
Nia whispered in
her head.
"I am inside of you."

As momma and daddy tucked Nia into bed, daddy asked her, "Did you find God today, my sweet child?"

She whispered as her heavy eyelids began to close, **"All around us and inside of us."**

O God, You have examined my heart and know everything about me.
You know when I sit down or stand up.
You know my thoughts even when I'm far away.
You see me when I travel
and when I rest at home.
You know everything I do. You know what I am going to say even before I say it, God. You go before me and follow me.
You place Your hand of blessing on my head.
Such knowledge is too wonderful for me, too great for me to understand!
I can never escape from Your Spirit!
I can never get away from Your loving presence!
If I ride the wings of the morning, if I dwell by the farthest oceans,
even there Your hand will guide me, and Your strength will support me.

–Psalm 139

Author, Adelia Davis

Adelia is from Detroit, Michigan and has always enjoyed creating stories. As a little girl, she would scribble stories down in her journal, act them out with her dolls, and tell them dramatically to friends and family. Today, she still shares children's stories with kids in her community and writes poetry. She is the founder and president of Story Shifters LLC, which offers volunteer youth programming and literacy resources focused on positive representation of Black people.
Adelia currently lives in Chicago, Illinois.

Illustrator, Zoe Black

Zoe is a lifelong doodler from Indianapolis, Indiana. Growing up, she loved reading almost as much as she liked drawing what she thought the characters would look like. Her first memorable encounter with the power of storytelling was in second grade, where her teacher's reading curriculum intentionally centered kids of color to mirror the diverse classroom.
Zoe currently lives in Brooklyn, New York.

CPSIA information can be obtained at www.ICGtesting.com
Printed in the USA
LVIW012241110221
679112LV00010B/65